Hats

PUFFIN BOOKS

Dear Parents

This book can be enjoyed by children of all ages. Younger children will enjoy and become familiar with the simple, repetitive phrases, encouraging them to "read" along with you. Older children, as beginner readers, will feel successful when they are able to read the simple, predictable text. Children of all ages will enjoy having fun with Barney and his friends.

We consider books to be lifelong gifts that develop and enhance the love of reading. We hope you and your child enjoy reading along with Barney!

Mary Ann Dudko, Ph.D.
Margie Larsen, M.Ed.
Early Childhood Educational Specialists

PUFFIN BOOKS

Published by the Penguin Group under licence from Lyons Partnership, L.P.
Penguin Books Ltd, 27 Wrights Lane, London W8 5TZ, England
Penguin Books USA Inc., 375 Hudson Street, New York, New York 10014, USA
Penguin Books Australia Ltd, Ringwood, Victoria, Australia
Penguin Books Canada Ltd, 10 Alcorn Avenue, Toronto, Ontario, Canada M4V 3B2
Penguin Books (NZ) Ltd, 182–190 Wairau Road, Auckland 10, New Zealand

Penguin Books Ltd, Registered Offices: Harmondsworth, Middlesex, England

First published in the USA by Barney™ Publishing, a division of Lyons Partnership, L.P. 1993
Published in Puffin Books 1995
10 9 8 7 6 5 4

Printed and bound in Great Britain by Saxon Profile Press

By Mary Ann Dudko, Ph.D. and Margie Larsen, M.Ed.

This is Barney's top hat.

Barney dances when he wears his top hat.
Imagine that!

This is Barney's cowboy hat.

Barney pretends to be a cowboy
when he wears his cowboy hat.
Imagine that!

This is Barney's fire hat.

Barney plays firefighter
when he wears his fire hat.
Imagine that!

This is Barney's artist's hat.

Barney paints when he wears his artist's hat.
Imagine that!

This is Barney's carnival hat.

Barney marches when he wears
his carnival hat.
Imagine that!

This is Barney's fishing hat.

Barney fishes when he wears his fishing hat.
Imagine that!

This is Barney's engineer's hat.

Barney drives a train when he wears his engineer's hat.
Imagine that!

This is Barney's crossing patrol hat.

Barney helps children
when he wears his crossing patrol hat.
Imagine that!

This is Barney's birthday hat.

Barney wears his birthday hat on his birthday.
Imagine that!

This is Barney's night hat.

Barney sleeps in his night hat.
Imagine that!

These are Barney's hats Barney likes all of his hats! Which hats do you like best?